MANDA HANSON *studied Calligraphy,*
Heraldry and Illumination at Reigate School of
Art. Now freelance, Manda has undertaken
many commissions including some for the
College of Arms.
Although Manda now mainly undertakes
commercial work, she has taught
part-time in Adult Education since leaving
College in 1985.

This book is dedicated to
Balavant & Daniel

Calligraphy

WORKSTATION

WORKSTATION *is a new concept comprising all the*
elements you need to start the art of Calligraphy.

Within the first 48 pages are alphabets and projects,
illustrated using the pens supplied in this kit, and an
additional 16 pages of grids are supplied at the back of the
book for practice work.

Manda Hanson

PRICE STERN SLOAN
Los Angeles

A PRICE/STERN/SLOAN – DESIGN EYE BOOK

© Design Eye Holdings Ltd.

Produced by Design Eye Ltd.
Published by Price · Stern Sloan, Inc.
11150 Olympic Boulevard,
Los Angeles, California 90064

ISBN 0 8431 3664 2

Printed in China
With Thanks to T. C. Li

Design Eye Ltd, 8 Fouberts Place, London W1V 1HH.

CONTENTS

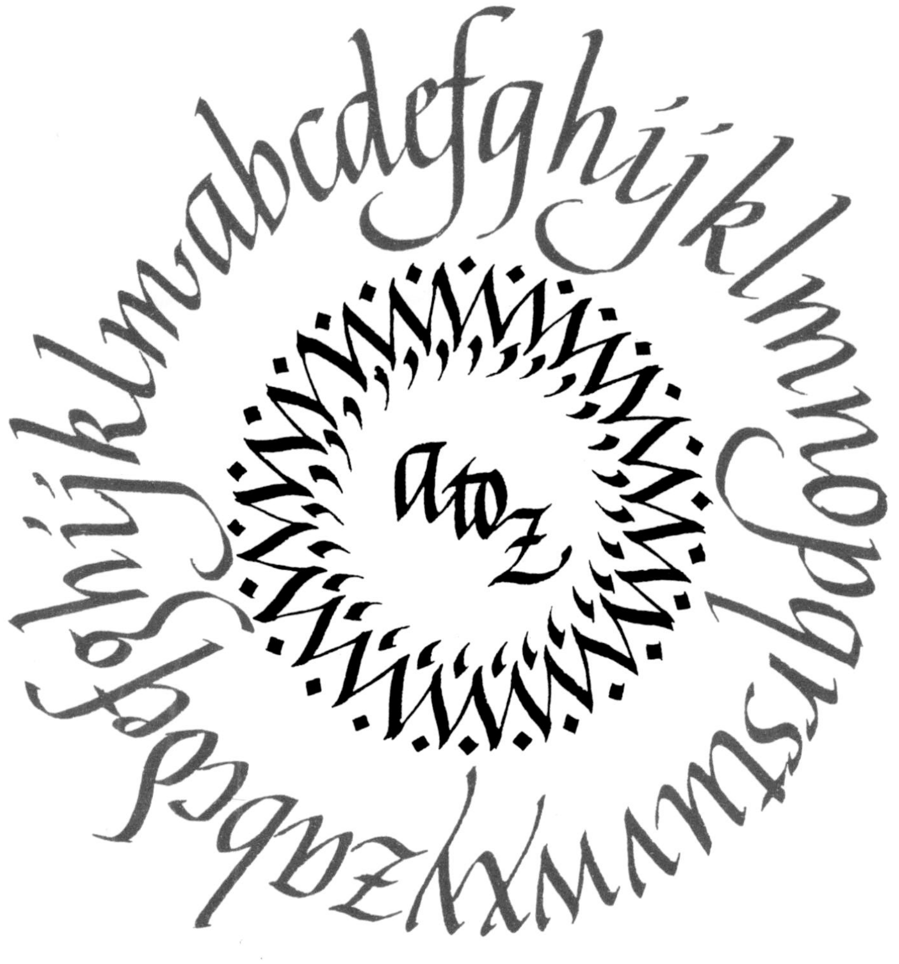
abcdefghijklmnopqrstuvwxyzabcdefghijklm
a to z

INTRODUCTION

*Calligraphy comes from the Greek **kallos**, beauty, **graphē**, writing – meaning 'beautiful handwriting'. When executed with the freedom and rhythm of a practiced hand, the result certainly can be 'beautiful writing'.*

There are many types and styles of writing, each calligrapher interpreting the same alphabet differently. This book introduces you to 4 different alphabets. First they can be copied, then practiced and finally interpreted in your own individual way. As long as the basic rules are followed, it is possible to produce your own 'beautiful writing'. Completing the special projects section of the book will help to familiarize you with the techniques and the various alphabets.

It has been said that to become a proficient calligrapher you should practice for 1 hour each day. To inspire you and encourage perseverance, there are some examples of my students' work amongst my own on pages 46-48 which emphasize how, with dedication, a beginner can produce outstanding results.

TECHNIQUES

E VERYTHING YOU NEED TO START practicing calligraphy is included in this work-station. At the end of the book you will find some practice pages which will help you develop your alphabets.

USING THE EDGED NIB

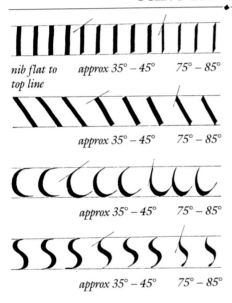

nib flat to top line   approx 35° – 45°   75° – 85°

approx 35° – 45°   75° – 85°

approx 35° – 45°   75° – 85°

approx 35° – 45°   75° – 85°

With the largest nib, draw some lines and curves, holding the nibs at various angles to the top line as shown. At first, you are merely discovering how different it feels to write with this pen rather than with a pointed nib or biro, which you are probably more used to.

PEN ANGLE

One of the most important things to concentrate on when starting out is the angle of the nib to the top of your writing line. When practicing an alphabet, it is the combination of the *angle* of the nib and the *direction* in which you pull it that controls the shape of the letter.

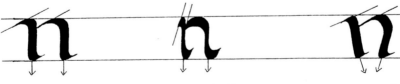

correct angle and direction of stroke.

wrong angle. The weight is in the wrong place.

correct angle but wrong direction of stroke.

To see the importance of the angle of the pen, fill in the squares on the right as shown. Start with the nib vertical to the top line and gradually decrease the angle. Notice how the inside shape changes as you go along.

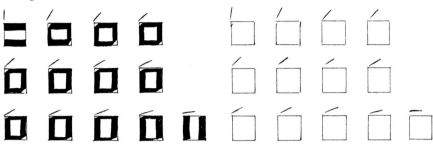

As the angle of the nib is changed from **|** *to* **▬** *so the shape of the letter can be changed.*

Now you can see how letters change if the nib is held at the wrong angle. Make sure you are relaxed and are holding the pen comfortably in your hand.

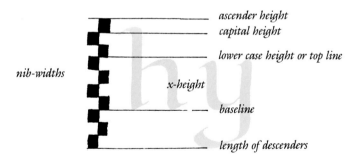

correct   too big an angle   too flat an angle

TERMINOLOGY

Here are some terms used to describe parts of the letters.

nib-widths

ascender height
capital height
lower case height or top line
x-height
baseline
length of descenders

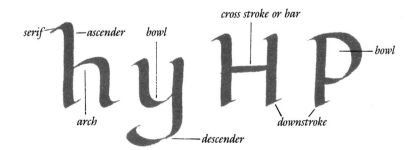

serif —ascender   bowl   cross stroke or bar   — bowl

arch   downstroke

descender

THE FOUNDATIONAL ALPHABET

R EMEMBER, WHEN YOU COPY AN alphabet you are imitating another calligrapher's version of it. After a little practice you will begin to create your own personal style.

The Foundational hand, which is simple and easy to read, is based on the alphabet devised by Edward Johnston early in this century. The nib should be held at an angle of 35° – 45° and the lowercase x-height is equivalent to 4 nib-widths.

In any alphabet you copy, always practice the letter 'O' first; all the other letters are based on this shape.

CCCCCCOOOCOO

This pattern is based on all the round-shaped letters obcdegpq.

mm ≡ ≡ ≡

Practice this for the ahmnrtuy.

VVVVVVVVVVV

Practice this for vwxy.

ƒƒƒƒ ƒƒƒƒƒƒƒ

This covers the letter 's'.

Practice the patterns on the left to get a feel for the letter shapes. Then practice the letters in the groups below; they follow a similar pattern and are constructed from similar strokes. Notice that for the letter 'z', you must flatten the angle of the downstroke.

bcdegopq   vwxy

ahmnuyrt   fijklsz z

The 'a' is the only letter of the alphabet where you do the right hand stroke first.

The cross strokes should be narrower from top to bottom than the down strokes are from side to side; this is only achieved if you are holding the pen at the right angle to the top line.

Keep an even distance inside the letter 'm'.

Make sure the first stroke of the 's' stays even throughout.

Start the 't' just above the top line otherwise it will look too small.

Keep the 1st and 3rd strokes and the 2nd and 4th strokes of the 'w' parallel – this will give a nice strong letter.

Remember to flatten the angle for the 2nd stroke of the 'z'.

Now try this simple exercise containing all the letters of the alphabet.
Remember to keep the width of the letter 'o' between each word.

sevenowildly panting fruit flies
gazed anxiously at the juicy
bouncing kumquat

FOUNDATIONAL CAPITALS

The capitals are 6 nib-widths high. Again practice the round 'O' first, keeping the nib at the same angle, between 35° – 45°.

Now copy the letters in the following groups. We start with the widest round letters, which are as wide as they are high.

All these letters should fit into a square.

Keep the horizontal stroke of the 'G' in line with the second stroke.

In the next group, the letters are slightly narrower.

These letters don't quite fit into a square and are more rectangular in shape. The 'Z' is made in exactly the same way as the lowercase 'Z', by flattening the angle on the down stroke. Take good care to check the position of your cross strokes. For instance the cross stroke on the 'H' is approximately halfway down or slightly higher, but never below this level, or the letter will give the appearance of being upside down!

The letters below are roughly half the width of the round 'OQCDG'. The 'P' is the only letter whose curve joins its stem more than half way down.

BEFKLPRS

The remaining letters are 'I' and 'J' which are only the width of the stem, and 'M' and 'W', which are the widest letters of the alphabet. The 'W' is made by joining two 'V's' together.

Try the following exercise, using only capitals, with the width of a capital 'O' between each word.

PACKOMY BOX WITH FIVE
DOZEN LIQUOR JUGS

SPACING

SPACING CANNOT BE MEASURED. Good spacing can only be achieved with a practiced eye. It is purely familiarity with the letter shapes and strokes that improves the spacing of letters.

Here are a few simple exercises to try, using the Foundational alphabet that you have already practiced.

There should be a similar width between each letter and inside the letter (the counter).

illumination

One basic rule to remember is that two straight strokes should be further apart than a straight stroke and a curve and two curves should be even closer together.

a curve & a straight stroke   *two straight strokes*

two curves

Watch out for combinations of letters, such as 'ra' and 'va'. Usually these have to be pushed together as closely as possible.

Move 'a' closer and shorten top serif.   *Move 'a' closer as before*   *Move 'l' closer and shorten top of 'f'.*

The width between two straight strokes should be similar to the width inside the letter. This applies to most alphabets.

mum   mum   m u m   mum

Blackletter   *Gothic Cursive*   *Foundational*   *Italic*

Practice these words, which have combinations of the letters on the previous page.

Now look at the sentences you practiced earlier and see where you could have improved the spacing. Remember, it is only by being able to see your own mistakes that you will greatly improve your calligraphy. There should be an even distribution of black and white space both between the letters and within the letter. The space between the words should be roughly the width of an 'o'.

mum|o|dad

Allow approximately two line spaces between writing lines.

happy

sad

Make sure that the ascenders and descenders do not overlap. If they should happen to do so, however, it is always possible to make a decorative feature out of them.

ꝚTALIC

THIS IS ONE OF THE most beautiful and versatile of all the alphabets. Try to hold the nib at a slightly larger angle than that used for the Foundational, approximately 45°. Do not make the angle too large as you will be inclined to distribute the weight in the wrong part of the stroke.

Foundational   Italic   correct   incorrect

Italic is constructed in a different way from the Foundational. Try these flow exercises without lifting the pen off the paper.

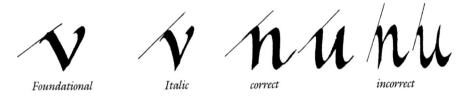

Again, with this alphabet, it is very important to get the shape of the letter 'o' right. Once you are familiar with the letter 'o', practice the letters in the following groups.

'c', 'e' and 'o', above, are all made in two separate strokes. The letters on the left are all similar in shape and, apart from the letter 't', are all made in one stroke.

bpbp bpbp bpbp

'b' and 'p' have similar contours; 'b' is made in one stroke and 'p' in two, springing the second stroke out of the first.

adgq adgq adgq

These four letters have the same contours and are made in two strokes except for 'd', which is made in three.

xyvw xyvw xyvw

'x', 'v' and 'w' are similar strokes. Make sure the 1st & 3rd and 2nd & 4th strokes of 'w' are parallel, the remaining letters do not follow any pattern, and can be made in more than one stroke.

f i j k l s z

au a b c d d de

ff gy g hijklm

no ppp qy q rs

tu vw x y y g z

hmn px z ks bb

Using the minuscule alphabet, try this sentence:

daveoquickly spotted the five women dozing in the jury box

Try to remember all you have learned from the spacing exercise and apply it to this alphabet also.

The Italic minuscule only appears to be joined up because the ends of the stroke are extended and overlapped. For example:

a c d e h i k l m

acdehiklm

Don't worry if the Italic leans to the right (forwards), it can be quite attractive when it does so. It is when it leans backwards that it doesn't appear so good!

ITALIC CAPITALS

These Italic capitals are quite similar to the Foundational capitals, but are based on an oval 'O'. Remember to keep the pen at an angle of 45°.

OOOOOOO   O   O

45°   30° – too flat   80° – too sharp

45°   30°

T T   E E E

For some of the horizontal strokes, you may find it easier to flatten the angle, so that the cross bars do not look too heavy.

Z Z

However, it is not necessary to change the angle for the 'Z'.

Try this exercise, using only capitals.

THE QUICK BROWN FOX JUMPS OVER
THE LAZY DOG

Try ranging the x-height of the lower case and the capitals. Remember,
the capitals are 2 nib-widths taller.

again again again CAPS

CAPS CAPS again CAPS

FLOURISHES

FLOURISHES ARE VERY ATTRACTIVE, BUT must be used sparingly and thoughtfully to achieve the best effect. They must only appear as extensions of the letterforms and must not in any way interfere with the shape and character of the letter.

Give the flourishes plenty of room. If they are too tight they will look awkward.

Do not alter the shape of the letter.

A badly shaped letter with flourishes; it is hard to tell what it is.

Nice straight flourishes that add length to the letter.

Badly formed flourishes that alter the shape of the letter.

Keep the flourishes open. Keep the strokes straight.

LINE ENDINGS

These are mostly used on the lower case letters and can be very useful when you need to fill a gap, or make a line of poetry appear longer.

FLOURISHES ON DESCENDERS & ASCENDERS

*Make sure the pen is flowing well and there is
plenty of ink before attempting this flourish.*

The man in the wilderness said to me
How many strawberries grow in the sea?
I answered him as I thought good
As many red herrings as grow in the wood

This 4-line verse makes use of all the flourishes you have learned.
Flourished capitals mark the start of each line. Flourished ascenders and
descenders add attractive detail to the words and line endings are used to
fill gaps where necessary.

GOTHIC BLACKLETTER

BLACKLETTER REFERS TO THE STYLE of the writing and Gothic refers to the period it dates from. It is mainly a decorative alphabet, not really being legible enough to be used for a large body of text. To get into the swing of this alphabet, the following exercises will be useful. Keeping the nib angle at about 35°, start by drawing some parallel lines 10 nib-widths high. Now reduce the height, first to 5 nib-widths and then to 7 nib-widths.

Practice the letter 'i' and the letter 'o'. The counter of each letter is approximately the width of a stroke of the letter.

Note the slight overlap.

Practice the letters in these groups. They all start with the similar first stroke; note how the second stroke is slightly elongated to give the letter its correct shape.

 *2nd stroke elongated*

This next group has similar strokes and endings.

The last group are the remaining letters, made up of dissimilar strokes.

Practice the word 'minimum'; it is a good spacing exercise.

Practice the following groups of letters, looking at the alphabet on page 24.

'mnharz' can also be drawn as shown on the left.

Try the following sentence, bearing in mind that there is approximately the width of a letter stroke between and inside each letter.

the five boxing wizards jumped quickly

BLACKLETTER CAPITALS

These letters are quite complicated and not very practical to use on their own. They are best used in conjunction with lower case letters.

GOTHIC   Gothic

Always start with the left hand side of the letter and work around it. The letter 'C' needs to be practiced quite thoroughly before you undertake any of the other letters. Remember to keep a nice round shape, slightly similar to the Foundational.

Practice the following groups of letters.

The decoration on Blackletter capitals is always added last. To create a thin line, turn the nib on its side so that it is vertical to the top line. The decorative side strokes are produced as shown on the left.

GOTHIC CURSIVE

THIS IS MADE IN A similar way to the Italic but has very different characteristics.

Italic 'o'   Gothic Cursive 'o'

This alphabet needs to be written quite quickly to achieve the character of the lettering. It can be written at 3 or 4 nib widths for the lower case and 5 or 6 nib widths for the capitals.

For this stroke the pen is held at 45° and turned until it is 90°. The same applies for the 'p'.

this is an 'r'.

GOTHIC CURSIVE CAPITALS

These capitals are very similar to the Blackletter; all you have to do is to lower the x-height to 6 nib widths. Remember always to start with the left hand side of the letter (except for the letter 'A'), and work your way around.

Versals

Versals are very decorative initial letters. They look very attractive at the start of a block of text. Generally speaking, they are not used to write whole sentences.

Versals are drawn with a pen (usually the smallest nib available) or brush and can be outlined in one color and filled in with another. They are basically constructed of a straight or round stroke, with hairline serifs running across the top and bottom of the strokes. Note how the straight strokes are slightly waisted just below the center.

approx 3 nib-widths wide

Letters can be filled in.

Versals can be any height.

ABCDEF
GHIJKLL
MNOPQ
RSTUVW
XYZÆO

To form the straight letters, always start with the left hand side, followed by the right hand side and lastly the serifs. These are made by keeping the nib at a flat angle to the top line. For rounded letters, always form the inside first, this will help to keep the shape strong.

LOMBARDIC VERSALS

These are based on a circle, and are usually wider than they are high. Form them in the same way as the Versals.

Here are some variations of Lombardic Versals.

Numbers &
Punctuation

N UMBERS CAN BE ADAPTED TO suit each alphabet. They can be as large as the capitals, the same size as the lower case, or somewhere in between.

1234567890

Foundational, Italic and Gothic numbers can be any x-height.

Here are numbers in various styles to supplement the alphabets you have already learned, plus a group of the most common punctuation marks.

1234567890

Foundational

1234567890

Italic

1234567890

Gothic

?!'";:;.()iíí

WRITING A QUOTATION

YOU WILL NEED A LAYOUT pad (A3 size), scissors, glue, a sheet of cartridge paper and the largest nib in the set. Copy the following text on the layout pad, using the Foundational Alphabet.

To me, old age is always fifteen years older than I am

Cut the text into strips and experiment with the arrangement until you are satisfied with the layout, then stick the strips down.

To me, old age is always fifteen years older than I am

All the writing lines are centered on this line.

In order to center the lines in the illustration above, fold the pieces of paper in half so that the first letter is over the last letter.

The final paste-up is used as a ruling guide for the finished piece. Transfer the baseline, topline and capital line measurements onto the cartridge paper. If you feel it necessary you can transfer the ascender and descender lines also. If you feel confident enough not to do this, just make sure the ascenders and descenders are even in length and do not fight each other.

Transferring guide lines

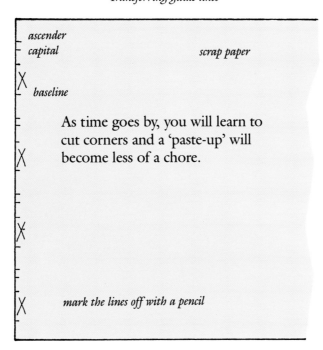

DOUBLE PENCILS

DESIGN A MONOGRAM

D OUBLE PENCILS ARE GREAT FUN to use, and can be used to form some impressive-looking letters. You will need two HB pencils, sharpened and even in length, and two elastic bands. Tie the pencils together, using one elastic band at the top and one near the tips. Now, using them just as you would a pen (the two points of the pencils are either side of the nib), hold them at the same angle as you would a pen and draw some letters.

abcdefghijklmnop

qrstuvwxy&z

ABCDEFGHIJ

KLMNOQPRST

UVWXYZ

Once you have decided on the version you like, you can decorate the inside with dots, lines or squares in a different color. The capitals I have used are Italic, but Blackletter capitals or even versals could be used.

For Italic flourishes refer to page 19.

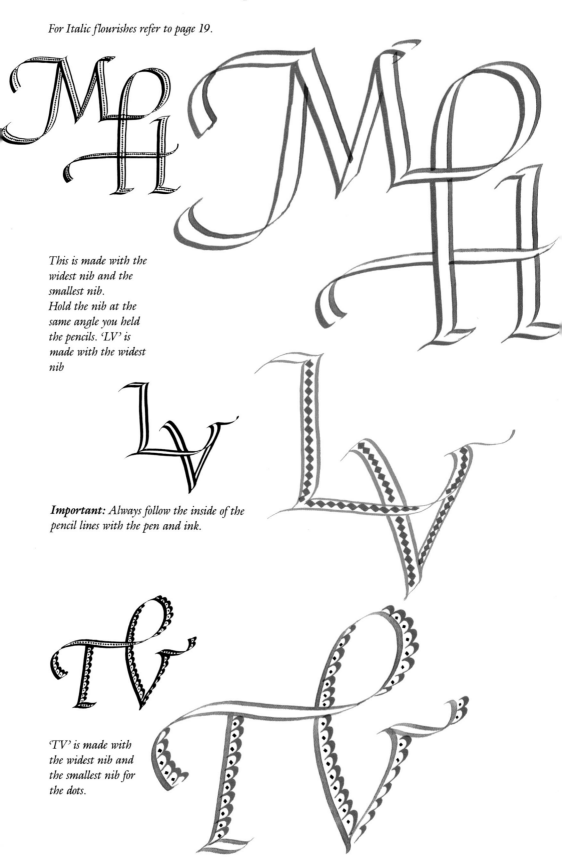

This is made with the widest nib and the smallest nib.
Hold the nib at the same angle you held the pencils. 'LV' is made with the widest nib

Important: *Always follow the inside of the pencil lines with the pen and ink.*

'TV' is made with the widest nib and the smallest nib for the dots.

Writing in a Circle

Writing in a circle looks very attractive, but it is a little harder than you might think! You will need a compass, some layout or cartridge paper, an HB pencil and a medium nib.

Draw a circle with the compass. Measure the height of the letters. Mark this on the circle and draw another circle on the outside.

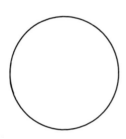

5 nib-widths

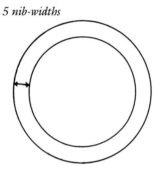

All the writing should radiate towards the center. You will need to draw some lines through the center of the circle and across the writing lines.

Now you can begin to write out the alphabet. If you feel very adventurous, you can draw another smaller circle inside and write some patterns in a different color.

These circular designs are a very good idea for a quick greeting card, substituting the alphabet for 'Happy Birthday' or 'Christmas Greeting', repeated around the outside.

WRITING IN A SPIRAL

ONCE YOU HAVE MASTERED THE circle, you can attempt the spiral design, which is quite complicated to form. The Foundational is a good alphabet to use for this. You will need: layout or cartridge paper, HB pencil, a protractor and a ruler.

Start by drawing a line halfway across the paper and mark off two points (1 and 2), approximately 1cm (¹/₂″) apart.

Put the compass point on mark number 2 and the pencil point on the other mark and draw a semi-circle above the line. Now, put the compass point on mark number 1 and the pencil point on the edge of the semi-circle and draw a circle underneath.

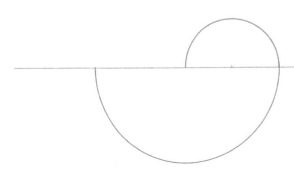

Basically all you are doing is swapping the compass point between marks 1 and 2 and opening up the radius as you go.

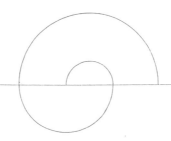

To draw a top line for your text, measure the height of the letters, mark it next to number 1 mark, placing the compass point on mark number 2. Put the pencil point on the new mark (number 3) and proceed to draw the spiral as before.

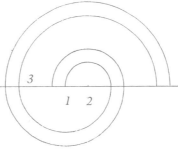

Again, as with the circle, you must bear in mind that all stems of the letters should radiate towards the center.

DECORATIVE BORDERS

DECORATIVE BORDERS ARE AN ATTRACTIVE and useful way of livening up a block of text. The hardest part of border design are the corners, sometimes it may be preferable to block the decoration or design a different corner.

Writing the patterns in blocks is easier then trying to design the corner. However, making a feature of the corner looks quite attractive.

Draw a baseline and a top-line on layout paper and, using the largest pen, start your border by writing a sequence of the same letter in a style of your choice. Then build up the border by adding punctuation marks (periods, commas, etc.), other decorations and color.

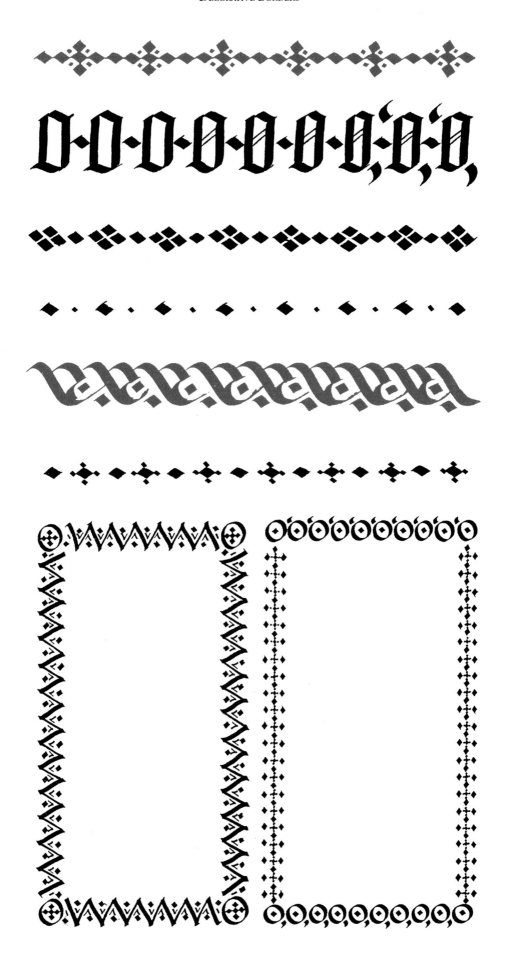

DESIGNING A BOOKPLATE

BOOKPLATES IF DESIGNED IN BLACK & white can be photocopied time & time again for your own personal library. They will identify your books when lent to friends.

Bookplates can have the Latin words *ex-libris* which means 'from the library of' or simply 'This book belongs to'.

When designing a bookplate do some small thumbnail sketches and when you have a design you like use the paste up technique described in the first project.

For a really decorative design you could incorporate the patterns shown in project 5.

If you require a large number of labels, it is a good idea to have them printed on gummed paper. However, if you only want a few, they can be written individually and pasted into books with a water based glue.

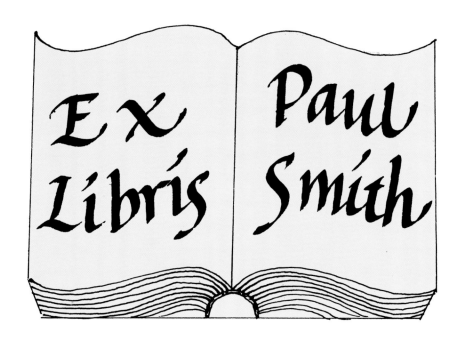

Words can be spaced out and closed up to fill the space available.

*Shorten or lengthen
the scroll to fit the
name.*

*There are some shield
shapes at the end of
the book which can be
used for bookplates.*

NAME PLAQUE

THIS IS A VERY USEFUL project as it can be used as a picture or a card. It also makes a delightful gift.

You will need some green and red ink, gold gouache paint, a small paintbrush, a suitable sized nib; a mapping pen and some ivory card.

Using the various oval shapes provided at the back of the book, draw an outside oval in pencil and some baselines for the names and dates. Here are some layout ideas.

Always pencil the lettering in lightly first. It is better to use Italic as it is easier to use on a curve. Then, write the name and date, making sure that the nib you use is appropriate to the size of oval you have chosen.

It is always nice to illustrate the picture. For a plaque, there is plenty of scope. Behind the name, very lightly pencil in the foliage. Go over it with the green ink and the mapping pen and then add some dots of color around it.

Lastly, draw and then paint, the central illustration. If you have some gold gouache, you can add gold dots to the foliage and to the lettering.

ILLUMINATED PANEL

THIS IS QUITE AN ADVANCED project which you should only attempt once you have practiced all the alphabets and feel more confident in your abilities. It also involves some painting.

You will need: gold gouache, green and red ink, a mapping pen nib and a piece of ivory card or mottled antique effect paper approximately 16 x 26 cms. For the calligraphy, use a small nib and black or brown ink. Gothic Cursive is the style of lettering used.

Firstly, using the grid at the back of the book transfer the measurements onto your sheet of card/paper. Write out the verse – the calligraphy is always done first in case of any mistakes.

The next step is the illustrated letter. Paint the background red first. Then, add the gold outline, gold piligree work and add patterns on the letter.

here is a gar-
den in her
face Where roses and
white lilies grow; A
heavenly paradise is
that place Wherein
all pleasant fruits do
flow, There cherries
grow which none may
buy Till "cherry ripe"
themselves do cry.

THOS CAMPION

Now draw the border, using a mapping pen and green paint. Treat it as if it is a floral growth. Each side has a starting point, which can be defined with a gold dot. Build up the border with the green, red and gold paint as follows.

1. Draw the main stem.

2. Add leaves, making sure they grow out of the stem.

3. Add flowers on the end of stems.

4. Add red buds on leaves.

5. Add gold decoration. Also add it to starting point above.

THOS CAMPION

If you can't find an appropriate paper for this project, you can stain ordinary cartridge paper with some tea or coffee, by giving it a wash with a wide brush or stippling it with a small brush; you can even flick a toothbrush dipped in paint or tea to create a speckled background.

A CITRUS POMANDER

Years ago pomanders were made of precious gums and resins, these were myrrh, spikenard and ambergris. The fixatives used were civet, benzoin, storax and musk. Elizabeth 1st usually carried a pomander made of benzoin and amber-gris. Mary Queen of Scots owned a pomander made of silver which is displayed at Holyrood House, Edinburgh. Cardinal Wolsey used pomanders similar to the ones we use today, he carried his tied to his belt to keep away the odour of his parishioners & the smells from the street.

HOW TO MAKE A POMANDER

section orange into four with sticky tape. Sort out the cloves into whole or stars. Cover four sections with cloves, using the stars to edge the sticky tape. Shake the pomander in the paper bag with the cinnamon and orris root. For about 3 weeks put the pomander to dry out in a linen cupboard. Remove the sticky tape after a few days to avoid mould forming underneath. The ribbon can be pinned on as the pomander shrinks and the ribbon repinned when necessary.

ABOVE **'A Citrus Pomander'**
Manda Hanson
Using the pomander as a central design the calligraphy was written around it. Cloves and orange blossom decorate the border. The shape of the design is based on two circles overlapping each other.

LEFT **'December' Rajinda Panesar**
This is a piece of student work; this page is part of a complete book which has been bound and sewn. The initial D is gilded using gold leaf.

ABOVE **'William Shakespeare' Kit Walker**
This piece was designed using a grid for the lines, the capital and the border. The border was created in a similar way as that on page 45.

LEFT **'The Feathers of the Willow'**
Derek Porter
This was based on a grid, but slightly adapted to accommodate the lettering. Peacock feathers were used as the basis of the border.

The feathers of the willow are half of them grown yellow

Above the swelling stream :

And ragged are the bushes .

And rusty now the rushes .

And wild the clouded gleam.

ring back the singing and the scent of meadowlands at dewy prime Oh bring again my heart's content. Thou spirit of the summertime.

William Shakespeare

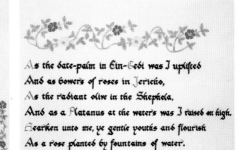

ABOVE **'Roses' Murray Wolf**

This is taken from a complete book about roses. The simple borders enhance the lettering adding interest to the subject.

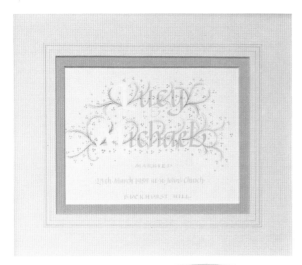

LEFT
'Wedding Plaque'
Manda Hanson
This is a very elaborate card. Taking just the names and decorating them.

BELOW
'Spiced Posies'
Manda Hanson
This lettering was designed so the writing would be continuous, the spiral method (project No. 4) was used.

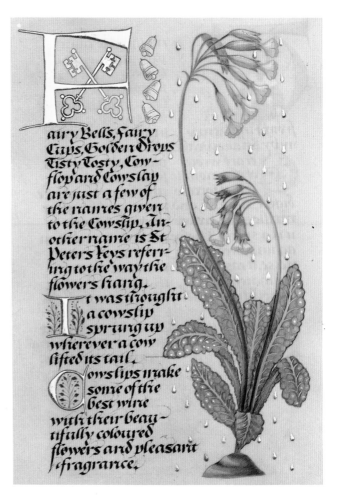

RIGHT AND BELOW
'Cowslip and Monkshood'
Manda Hanson
These two pages are part of a book project produced on vellum. Using the traditional method of gilding, the actual design is based upon 15th century style manuscripts.

BELOW RIGHT
'Oh to be in England'
Kit Walker
This lettering is uncials produced on a parchment style paper. Again a grid was used to get the balance of the border, capital letter and text correct.

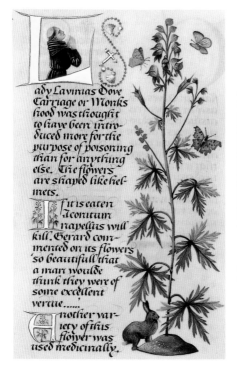

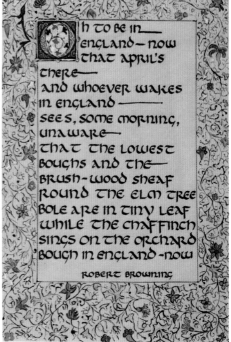

PRACTICE GRIDS

T HE FOLLOWING PAGES CONTAIN printed grids on which to practice your calligraphy. You will also find templates, which you will need for some of the projects.

GENERAL GRID – SMALL NIB

Foundational

abCg

Italic

abCg

Gothic Cursive

abCg

Foundational

abCg

Italic

abCg

Gothic Cursive

abCg

Foundational

abCg

Italic

adCg

Gothic Cursive

adEg

o Odg

oⵕⴰg

n O d g

A

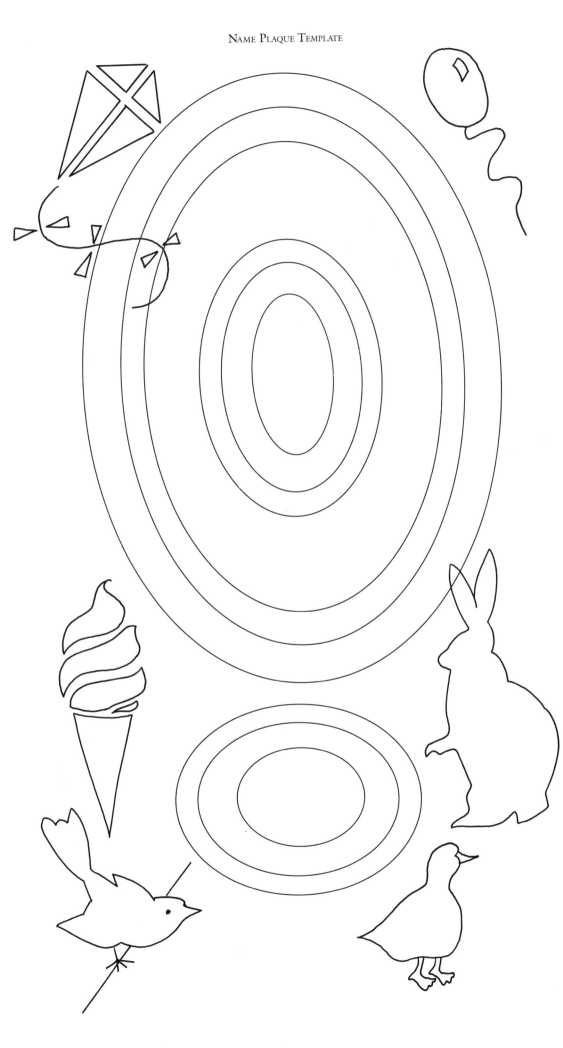

Illuminated Panel Grid

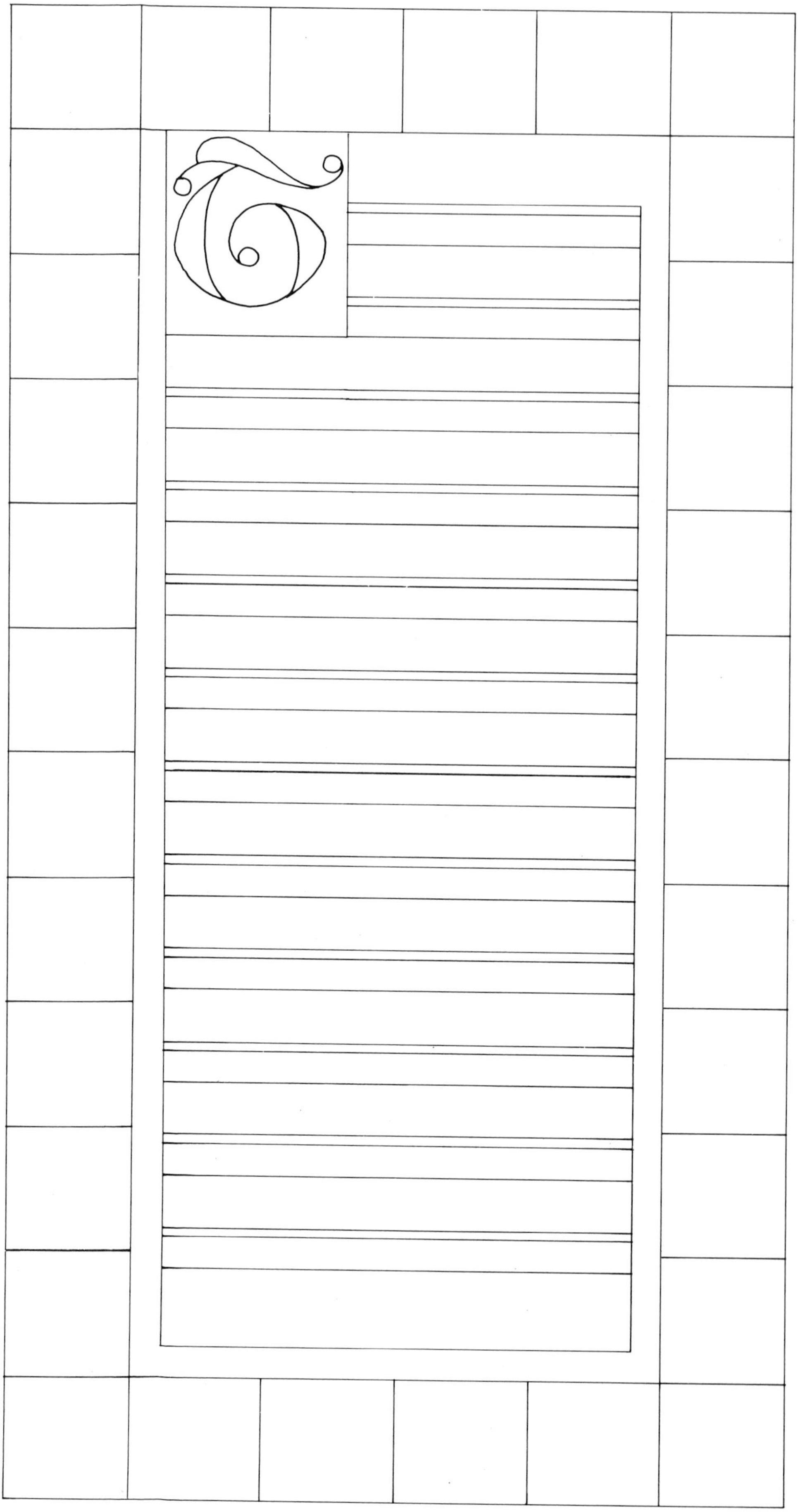